PURPLE SOCIETY

Purple Society

O.K. Nay

CHAPTER 1

The last time such kind of event happened was a decade ago- it took forty-nine minutes; two minutes to rob the place and the rest forty-seven as down-time while waiting for the getaway car. Dear citizens of Colorful first took notice at the forty-eighth minute when the robbers where stashing the wares in their truck. The police in their usual way blamed the people for complacency and non-vigilance; it only took the police fifteen hours to respond to the crime. Its true that's the shortest response time anyone in Colorful can recall, still the sense of timing in this town is absurd.

On this cool, drab, foggy morning, slowly appeared Iliy closely followed by Azeez, peeking from a lonely cashew tree that appears to be on the fence as it concerns the sinister design of the boys. Their teenage faces still bright and untendered by the harshness of the sun, focus sternly at the work ahead of them. Both surface from the covering of the tree, and only stop to wear woollen masks cut to allow them exercise the functioning of their eyes and mouth. Azeez had apprenticed with an abusive tailor for a time, and seeing no headway, decided to sell off the fabrics and dyes in the shop while his boss was away, as farewell. So he did the cutting of the masks.

They both walk past series of low-end stores; at this time of the day, many residents are just feeling the warmth of their bed, so it makes good business sense to stay 'Closed' till mid-afternoon. There is no inspiration to do otherwise. Both stop on getting to the entrance of Madam Social General Store.

Even though the store is only the one open, they target the store because along with Mama Sunshine's Joint, no other store in town run on cash, they are accommodating to barter their goods. It goes this way: Ini & Sons Electrical Store put up a notice of a seldom used 14" TV in exchange for an item they notice a lack of around town- a bag of rice. If a rise in the value of television is anticipated, Papa Thiaroye's Farm will vie for it, it's harder to undertake otherwise. That's the main reason most stores in Colorful are homogenous in relation to one another, and the people here put other jack of all trades to shame.

Iliy has the wind taken off his sails after a slight incident involving him and the glass door coming together. Azeez is taken aback.

"Get a grip," said Azeez.

Azeez must have made both masks with his measurement, with no care for Iliy's large hazel eyes. Both are now in Madam Social's line of sight. Azeez belatedly charge forward, he draws out a pistol from his washed out brown jacket and hesitantly points it at her.

"Your money or your ...never mind, all I want is your money," Azeez bargained, "please."

Iliy joins the stick-up. "What!" Iliy surprised at Azeez's plea. "Step aside. Cooperate with us and we'll go easy with you."

Madam Social can't be fooled by the up starters. As if her ears were shut. She stares at them the same way a billboard model looks undeterred at passers-by, where the model manages to keep eye contact with a lot of people at the same time. The boys can feel themselves shrink in size from her look. It was recorded on her that her days were unbearable.

"Iliy is that not you?" asked Madam Social.

Iliy is up to the task. "Listen, it will be safer if you don't get to know us."

Madam Social gets chilly and it shows in her voice. "Azeez, do you know that you were putting on those same clothes on your last day of work here?"

"You've got me confused for someone else ma'am, someone

else can easily own one of these," Azeez said defiant.

"The Sahara desert has more people there than this cold town, what are the chances anyone will have a custom jacket with words 'Young & Restless', I'd like to see that," said Madam Social.

She ignored to comment on Iliy's white, clean, fitted T-shirt. It's unfair to Iliy that Azeez's carelessness get to decide how the hustle gets botched; playing a subordinate role in his own life.

The boys don't argue with her, because they did not feel strongly enough about the robbery. Both relent and follow Madam Social eyes and hands instructions when they humbly rest their pistols on the glass counter. Madam Social turns her attention to their new fascination.

"Where did you get these?" asked Madam Social.

"At the toy shop," they chorused.

"I know your faces are not made from wool," she reminded them.

Even in their dejected state, the masks still gave them a layer of dignity. They take off their tight-fitting masks to reveal the new folds on their faces. Both set the masks on the table. They only elevate their hunched heads after a resounding double thwack from Madam Social. She set them off.

The boys are thrown back on the street. The whole event lasted for about three and a half minutes. It takes longer than that for the people of Colorful to take notice.

"Let's take on the highway, rather than sticking-up our former places of work," said Iliy weak from trying to meet up with Azeez.

Azeez is more built, with more scars to show.

"Keep your ideas to yourself," said Azeez in disgust. "There is a reason we hold up only familiar places..."

"Oh I know..." Iliy retorted.

"Do you?" Azeez restored his position. "Do you have any know-how on robbing buses you'd like to share? If it's not broken don't fix it, I am not going on any highway that will most likely lead to the grave."

Iliy does not relent. "I have got to leave this town one way or the other, and the highway seems like a good place to start that journey. I have it all figured out."

Azeez have known Iliy all his life to understand that such equivocal arguments can never be remedied in a lonely township road, so he leaves Iliy to brood.

"Azeez!"

CHAPTER 2

The sun is shining its usual rate, and taken a position aside Iliy, who is resolved to spend the rest of his time underneath the resplendent mango tree reading his three year old fashion magazine.

Counting his steps, Azeez makes a spot for himself a stretch from Iliy.

"What do you plan to do?" asked Azeez.

It's ten in the morning in a dusty, calm, patched road. For its condition it can be mistaken for an old dirt road plied by men on saddles; it links half the country to the Capital city about two hundred miles away. The launch of airports in major cities has vastly removed the need to mend roads, leading to the Capital city making it clear that people who can't fly to them are 'Undesirable guests'.

That's how Mama Sunshine puts it.

A luxurious coach appears in the horizon. One had to come through eventually- they've been here the past three hours. The boys step out of the thicket in masks with pistols pointed at the unsuspecting driver. They make their way into the bus. The complete silence and puzzled glances from the frightened passengers, reassures the boys that they are off to a good start.

"You already know what it is," said Azeez, "so you'll do well to hand over what you've got to me and my colleague!"

Iliy collects from the left side of the bus, leaving Azeez the other. No fuzz or hard remarks from the abundant passengers. The boys are mostly interested in their provision of cash, anything else will be impossible to fence in Colorful. A mean lady center of the fairly new bus refuses to part with her bag.

Iliy approaches her with no malice in mind. "Ma'am won't you see it as investment in the future?" Iliy try to coax her.

She has no interest in what she is not going to be part of, her uneasy hands clutch tighter to the bag.

"Give me the damn bag!"

She does, scared. The rate of compliance from the rest improves tremendously after that. In this line of work be fast and adaptable.

They run out from the bus and head straight across the road carrying a high number of bags. They enter their less inspired car and aim to drive off. The white color of the Jetta have lost its brilliance, the sun's effort to exude some shine from the car is rejected. But it runs smooth. All the boys ever asked of a getaway car is be inconspicuous and run fast; they don't have the means to change its color so they settle for its speed.

The boys keep their system operational in a series of bus heist, but making sure they never threaten the use of their weapons on resistive ones, since they know the pistol is made for kids who'd like a taste of the Wild West; Iliy was prepared enough to get spare guns from the toy shop before they hit Madam Social's store. It cost them a week of offloading, packaging and delivering of store items to customers of Playtime's toy shop.

Azeez's poorly-white teeth are wide open but his is just one of the few decent showings, as the passengers revel in Iliy's jokes.

The oncoming bus is the smallest they've encountered but the sun will soon give in to night. Inside were old and disavowed people. The boys get them to line-up at the side of the bus. It's horrible.

"This is worse than staying at home," said Iliy.

In a short while, Azeez stands at the door of the bus handing their loots to these lots who seem to have had it harder in life than them. Iliy helps the harried ones back to the bus. This act gives them no sense of well-being; it means they have to double their effort in the days to come.

On a new day and at the usual place, a luxurious bus is stopped by Azeez and Iliy still concealed by their masks and wielding their pistols. The driver humbly let them in.

"Try to remain your calmest, we will be out of your way as quickly as we came," Iliy assured them. "Pass what you have with you to us."

The bus is serene and devoid of stress. No grumblings. A steadfast lady stares at them.

"Iliy, is that you?" asked Edna.

Her silky voice is all too familiar to Iliy. He turns to her, rekindling the flame that has burnt brighter than any he ever had; while her skin glistens underneath her pallid gown, her glassy eyes are covered with reflection of bemused Iliy. She left him for technical college.

Azeez in wide-eyed despair witness the dishonor done him by his friend. Iliy takes off his mask in haste, grabs Edna and for a moment muse about a place in the stars made for them.

"Edna!"

"What's your problem man?" Azeez chided.

"Is that Azeez I hear?" asked Edna.

Azeez's fate has being tied to Iliy's for as long as he has come to know himself. He put up no defense. Edna springs toward Azeez and clutch him in a hug that he partakes in unexcited. The robbery is delayed for the mean time, and the mystified passengers will have to make room for these strange fellows.

"What are you guys doing, I mean is this what you guys do now?" wrapping her words in condescension, picked up by Azeez.

Iliy develops the ability to dull most senses in favor of one- he sees his world take shape in her.

"You mean highway robbers right?" inferred Azeez.

Iliy come round to reason. "Is that what you think of us?" asked Iliy. "We are in practice for our next show. We are trying our act on an unwilling audience."

Edna gets a sense that he is not honest. "This is all staged? It looked so real some seconds ago," maintained Edna.

"Sure. We aim to push ourselves, no matter where it takes

us," said Azeez.

Mixed reactions trail their escapade, some still see the heat brewing in Azeez's crooked eyes; barely hiding the fact that he doesn't like the new direction this robbery is going.

"I'm impressed," said Edna.

"How come I never get you on the phone?" asked Iliy.

"I switched with one of the newer networks- I can't remember which one," replied Edna.

"You think there is a way we can hang out later? We have a lot to catch up on."

"That is not possible," said Edna unflinching.

"Why not, we can make arrangements, I missed you- didn't you miss me?" Iliy let escape a bit of desperation.

Azeez close his mind to their dilly-dallying, he wonders how he can see broadly the things to come and can't pull the plug. Was he disarmed by her charm too?

"I've got my family to think of," said Edna.

Iliy had suspected the glint bearing on his eyes cannot all just be from her fair skin or her sparkling pert lips, the ornaments is culpable for that, one of her left finger is of relevance to Iliy and its filled.

In the meantime Azeez shakes off his fetters.

"Who?" asked Iliy.

"Drop it Iliy," said Azeez.

Iliy turns his bloodshot eyes to him, he can only take one stab in the back at a time, Azeez learns to fall behind.

"Ok. Go on," Iliy insisted.

"Bashir. He works at the mill you know, just like me- and in a position of authority too, just like me," said Edna.

"Of all the guys in the world, it had to be him, eh," said Iliy.

The engrossed passengers silently question each other's motive; they don't know who among them is another planted actor.

"You know how much I hated him in school," said Iliy.

"Do you have kids for him?" Azeez fan the ember of discord.

"A boy and a girl," she said almost in anger.

Iliy can't take more of this love story turn sour. He takes her bag forcefully from her.

"Show's over everyone!" announced Azeez, without much surprise from the passengers.

Azeez quickly resumes collecting the bags of the other passengers.

CHAPTER 3

Azeez and Iliy are looking at a poster on the wall declaring them wanted. The poster isn't well detailed. The picture on display does in fact portray the boys in their adolescence, with their names in full- even though in this town people rarely recall anyone except by nicknames. The boys are only clearly shown in inelegant poses; Iliy's left hand that is supposed to be around someone is cut off, Azeez is leaning to the right on no support. A figure at the center of frame has been cut out. Their smile is so sincere and adorable; happier times. The reward money is the first Colorful has ever seen. They've never had to sell out their own, even if the kids in the poster don't look familiar.

Colorful in its beginning was a city deemed to take a pivotal position in the affairs of the country; 'City of the future' the Daily Sun declared; 'Confluence city' as aptly termed by early voyagers for linking major parts of the country to the Capital city.

A steel mill was built in the city when Iron ore was discovered here. The people dignified themselves in their work and opened their doors for their fellow countrymen to flourish. It wouldn't take long for the oil boom and a new government to come on board. The government could no longer justify to itself why industrial complexes need be built to make products from this processed steel- nobody in Colorful could really understand it but the government cut off the steel plant completely.

The city was in limbo, not suspecting the worst was yet to come. It happened in a day like every other before it: pedestrian, remote and stifling, with no one paying attention to the encroaching brush and trespassing wildings; the land in effect turning green.

The rumble began at Papa Thiaroye's Farm; goats bleat in hope of warning the proprietor, chickens respond by testing their flight range.

A series of explosion will go on to rock the town. Twenty-seven minutes of pure carnage. The low death toll was credited to the dwindling population after the industrial shutdown. Our government was in no haste to salvage the situation. No official response would come for a long time.

Those were the early years of Mama Sunshine's Joint. It was here that the Grey Hat Society's involvement will take root. Largely considered a foreign intelligence agency, nobody knows much about the dark organization. They mostly gather intelligence from the shadows, and do so without mixing with the people. No foreigner has ever been seen wearing a grey hat in Colorful, Mama Sunshine insists they do so only at their embassy since they are on foreign soil.

The theory is that Our government had renege on a deal with theirs that will end the encroachment into neighboring countries by Our government. We had gone ahead to sign on to supply oil, and cement and electricity to over half the continent. These interests are of huge profit to these foreign powers, and most vital, they see losing it as a regression in the order and grip they lord over the continent.

So they hatched a perfect plan to undermine the country-bomb Colorful. Due to its previous occupation as a steel production center, a highly organized underground system was already in place. They can rig the forsaken industrial complex through this access way. It will show their hostile host how close they can get to the seat of power, and at anytime they can show their might if Our government refuses to follow directives. A stern repercussion.

Our government will go on to say later that the explosion was only due to detonation of abandoned explosives laid underground during the Civil War, and will apologize in passing for the government's oversight. Before then, Mama Sunshine has had three years to convince everyone in Colorful of her side of things of one of the most enduring event the people have ever known.

That was a long time ago nobody wants to remember, vestiges of that era are stuck underground, few still standing in defiance to the people's neglect.

CHAPTER 4

The air was very tense in the car on this fateful day. Iliy is scanning through the monthly periodical, especially at the crime segment. Azeez is thinking of a way to drive uphill and then leave the car volleying, tumbling back on to the highway with Iliy firm in his seat, and him having a laugh from the top of the hill.

"I don't think 'less privileged' is right," offered Iliy.

He takes no respite from Iliy's effort. Azeez grimaces.

"Hell fire- so if I'm not less privileged that means what?" continued Iliy.

Azeez permits his lips to part.

"You're privileged?" asked Azeez.

"Exactly- most people aren't in the first place, I mean... it's like a special right- right? For a few, others have none of it, then it's not less."

"Less might mean nothing in this situation. It's tricky," Azeez attempted to clarify.

Iliy tries to conceal his unease and disappointment in his well-meaning colleague. "Less is less, nothing... well is nothing!"

"It's not wrong boy! I am so much a less privileged youth, I mean I got some but I don't have near enough privilege," Azeez discard gentle persuasion.

Iliy is not motivated to pick up on Azeez's feeble argument; he drops the periodical to pick a tatty poster he took from the wall.

"The damn police could not even get recent pictures, I don't look that thin anymore," said Iliy.

"Damn her!"

"Pillock. Who cares how you look, we have to skip town as soon as frigging now," said Azeez.

Iliy gives in to the persistent wind howling at him, his face being slapped and embraced by the poster concurrently. The poster is left to flutter outside the car.

Another conversation starts to form in Iliy's mouth. Azeez wipes the little foam that has formed at the side of his mouth.

"How is he taking the loss?" asked Iliy.

"Better than I thought," Azeez said without hesitation.

Maybe he is not hearing clearly, Iliy thinks to himself. "I mean his wife."

"He told me how his life tragedies culminated in domestic life," Azeez said.

"He was with her for over fifty years bro," Iliy said still puzzled.

"Who's counting?" asked Azeez. "You can easily see the sincerity in his smile these days," Azeez slows down to cross a bump in the road. "Never had it easy as a child, abusive ne'er do well as parents, still he found the zest for life. Could have been a priest if not for the Second War," Azeez slows for another bump. "The Civil War was his last fellowship with men. He'd get married and feed on only what he grows."

"Poor woman," Iliy said shaking his head.

"Dreams she might have had," added Azeez.

Azeez stops again but this time it's urgent. A taxi suddenly park in front of them to drop a passenger, leaving Azeez angry.

"Mad man, you have wood in your eyes? Get off the way!" Azeez yelled.

A passenger alight from the car hurriedly, the lack of grace in his movement suspend Iliy's attention.

"Azeez," Iliy called, eyes wide open.

"What!" Azeez responded, transferring aggression.

Iliy understands. "I get it now."

"Get what?" Azeez asked.

"We have being sitting in paradise all this time and we didn't even know."

"Dear child, say what you have to say," Azeez reiterated and began driving.

Iliy taps on the dashboard, trying in vain to hit a good tune, or maybe he intend for the noise.

"This baby here," said Iliy. "Think about it, the difference between that guy and us right now is that we don't get paid, but he does for driving on the same road, you see it?"

Azeez reach for the brakes, again. The brake pad tried venting its frustration by leaving the car to go on, but it was made for the exact opposite, so it complies.

"Show me your permit. Do you have any idea where we can even get one?" Azeez asked.

Iliy starts to feel that he might have harbored this idea for a long time, it seems too familiar.

"But we don't need a permit, all we need to do is avoid going into town... those trips are most times short anyway, and less rewarding," explained Iliy.

Azeez tries to be more attentive.

"We just stick to the highway and carry passengers from city to city, more money," Iliy continued.

Azeez lends his voice again. He shouldn't be perceived clueless. "Ok, but this job requires just the driver, in this case me, have you thought of that?"

The day keeps getting brighter for Iliy, as he introduces a system to meet both halfway. "No way! In this business where there is no record how am I going to know what is made after a day's work. This car is as much yours as it is mine in case you can't remember," Iliy tries to eliminate Azeez's point as first measure.

"You don't trust me now?" Azeez try to tempt Iliy.

"I absolutely don't trust you and never will," Iliy won't be baited. "There is nothing new in it, you drive I conduct, or I will just pose as your passenger capiche! Whichever works."

Azeez starts the car. 'Capiche' is all new to him, he wonders whether it's a codeword, anagram, abbreviation; C.A.P.I.C.H.E. C for what?

CHAPTER 5

At the center of Colorful a church had been built, for the people to keep their Sundays in. And most did.

It has always bothered me why the boys never listen to the priest's annual predictions at the start of the year service. I know they know because the Notice Board has a dedicated section where the pamphlet containing the prophecies is placed all year long, and till now at least one of these predictions will turn out to be true; this year, a series of wild fires was prophesied to occur at the first quarter, lo and behold it did.

Mama Sunshine swore she heard the priest talk about a meeting he had with Our government and some business interests- logging business, heading to our town just the year before. If that gave the priest a heads up of what's to come or it's purely divine she can't be sure, because the wild fires started when they came to town. Same wild fires recorded in previous cities the said logging business plied their trade in.

The boys always have their noses raised whenever they pass the magnificent edifice of a church; Azeez is a boy with a long nose. It's the only time they get this way.

Iliy said he could see Jesus as his Savior but he can't concern himself to be in a room with people for the single reason of them sharing the same faith. Same way he never attends to the boys club. Azeez is afraid his association with the lovers of Christ might make him turn out like them- he wouldn't want to blame the devil for his woes, or his neighbor.

Petty excuses from the boys, but as good as any. They never

seem to contemplate things much before taking action.

CHAPTER 6

It was bright this morning in Colorful. Birds flew from the sky, and ascended.

A gray woman standing by the road with her goods waves down the white Jetta. Azeez stops eagerly, Iliy gets out to load her items into the car. She trades in ironware, and the blistering sun has stripped her of any patience she once had as she hurried in.

It's later in the day, and windy, soon it will be sunset. A passenger is getting ready for tonight's sleep as she naps in the backseat. Azeez propose that she will keep napping even past her stop, Iliy in rare fashion stands up for sleeping beauty. Maybe he considered the amount of potholes they will come across before her stop. A bit past half-way to her stop, the car jumps to a high degree making all three occupants bump their heads to the roof of the car. Azeez's knowledge of out-of-town bumps is not up to date. She stays awake through the rest of the way.

A home-made empty 14" cupboard is opened by Iliy to deposit the proceeds from the day.

The customers for some reasons always consider Iliy a fellow passenger; all fares are instinctively paid to the driver-Azeez. Iliy opts to take the development with accord and understanding. Thank goodness for his supersized eyes- they were always going to come handy at some point in his life; Iliy's peripheral vision is superb, hence he can feign checking out the bowing leaves out his window and yet give a precise account of what Azeez received throughout the day. Azeez never offer any amount that can be disagreed upon in his defense.

Iliy's importance is pronounced when conflicts arise between Azeez and the passengers. They are always looking to Iliy to stand in solidarity against the oppressive and extortionist driver Azeez. And Iliy never waste time in pointing out that the customers are always right.

The jaunty Mama Sunshine can't deny the feeling that something is amiss with the increased patronage from Azeez and Iliy. Even though her joint has been the only succor for all and sundry, leading to an undeniable influx of people every day, she can still rehash the names of everyone stepping into the place, but calling "Azeez" "Iliy" sends her tongue rolling into uncharted corners of her mouth.

The one person who might know enough to have set her at ease was on a self imposed hold-your-breath contest with her.

Madam Social rumor has it first came up with the idea of expanding her venture to include a joint filled with live music, bar and delicacies, which she divulged to her bosom friend Mama Sunshine. Little did she know that her doe-eyed tender friend has experienced an eye-opening revelation.

"Do you think the white color of our car has done us better?" asked Iliy about to gulp a glass of chilled beer.

Azeez shrugs while struggling with bones wedged between his teeth.

"I best ask the customers any chance I get," Iliy said to himself.

People have always confronted Mama Sunshine as to her unusual jubilation outside of Madam Social's porch on that day of the meeting. Comrade Jinaid, the funeral home director attested to seeing her jump twice in excitement which lifted his erstwhile gloomy disposition.

Of course Mama Sunshine doesn't deny leaving the regular teaching job she has known most of her adult life to the world of an entrepreneur, but she sees it as saving the people from impending monopolization fixed in the mind of Madam Social. And to make a lot of money while at it, this ill-mannered people always remind her.

Madam Social has vowed to never share the same air with her for the rest of her natural life. In this regard Mama Sunshine shows she's still up to the task. Through their careful network of spies, they both ensure to find out what the other is up to before going anywhere important. She might have boasted in daylight, but at night Madam Social knows her lungs are not the way they were in her younger days. Mama Sunshine really doesn't see any need in navigating the grueling marketplace half conscious.

Mama Sunshine keeps hope that one day, the tale of how the unsuspecting duo of Colorful came about their new found prominence will be made known to all. Working out of town definitely has its perks.

The cupboard serving as their cash box is almost filled with money. Tax-free, free of bank charges, union fee-free money.

On the road again, passenger side filled up, answering a questionnaire. The smiles on the faces of Iliy and Azeez have never been broader. They are forced to open their mouths in laughter to avoid cracking their lips. Their lives in a week.

CHAPTER 7

The continuity of the road is broken by a mirage; the white Jetta appears in a rush. A lone female passenger is sitting quietly at the back. She introduced herself to the boys as Ovi. She has her hairy arms crossed across her raised chest.

"Did the color of the car influence your decision to get in?" asked Iliy.

She takes her time, to add importance to what she has to say.

"I guess so."

"Why would that be?" Iliy inquired.

"You didn't paint it the usual color because you are either too cheap or you are working under the radar," she said, "so I thought you must be cheap anyways, worse you could be little devils, but that's not mostly the case in this town."

Coupled with the questionnaires, Iliy has his answer. The color does increase their visibility to customers.

The drudgery of the day has drained the excitement out of the day for the boys. The westerly sun seem to be teasing them, flashing its light at intervals as they drive across a dense vegetation of trees of varying sizes. Iliy is struggling with the allure of sleep.

In front is a police checkpoint manned by a frail, unfit police officer. The police officer flags Azeez down, which he obeys.

Azeez tries for a warm smile; he can't convince himself that the development is cordial as his lips twitches.

The policeman looks sternly at them for a while using one of the many tricks from the book to unnerve his prey. His eyes do not betray his intentions as they are shielded from engaging the eyes of others by a dark sunglass. The contours on his face are from previous vocations and his skin patches are creating a visual sore for the boys. And the girl.

"License and registration," demanded the policeman.

Azeez dutifully hand both documents to the policeman. The policeman pretends to check if the papers are in order, also exchanging glances with them at every point of his inspection; more of keep a watchful eye on them as the boys can't tell where his attention is held through that knock off dark sunglass. From the color of the car, the policeman intelligently asserted that the car is for personal gains, what else can white cars be used for.

"Who is the lady at the back?" the policeman smelled blood.

"Her? My niece- ehm Ovi," replied Azeez.

"Eh?" Ovi lets out in shock.

The policeman is interrupted by gusty winds that want to deprive him of the documents in his care.

Iliy quickly execute an idea. "You get a free ride the whole of today," Iliy offered Ovi.

Maybe it's their curt behavior to her all through the drive here, or an astute ability she's had before then.

"One month," Ovi proposed.

"A week," Iliy countered.

From the firmness of his eyes, his unshaken breath, she knows he has nothing more to give.

"Good afternoon officer," said Ovi.

"Is he your uncle?" asked the policeman.

"That's right sir," said Ovi jovially, "he just don't act like one most times."

"You look too young to be her uncle," the police officer said facing Azeez.

Ovi is unwelcoming of any conversation that will deprive her of the attention she just held. "His father, my grandfather saw it in his right to take a young bride," reestablishing her presence, "he was the resulting child of the said bride, while I was the first grandchild of the family. I think we were born a year apart."

The officer can't shake the smell of blood piercing through his nostrils.

"Hm. The both of you do look familiar though, how do I know you two?" the policeman addressed Azeez and Iliy.

"If you've ever been to a local theatre, you might have seen one of our shows… the 'Lost Boys of the Purple Ribbon Society'," replied Iliy.

The policeman is terribly out of sorts. He hand the papers back to Azeez and knocks on their car signifying they can leave. They move slowly up the rest of the way, until he policeman disappears out of their world.

They revel in retaining their freedom. The familiar air of excitement is accompanied by a loud combination of laughter from the boys. Ovi checks her bag and brings out two flyers and hands it to both of them. Iliy squeezes his and puts it in his pocket- the aftertaste of their agreement puts him in a bad light. Azeez tries to read while driving, counting his words.

"The Boulus-Family-Blasting-Company, supply factory-size dynamites, custom-made…" he become frustrated, "to hell with this," he lets the flyer take a place on the dashboard until he can ascertain what kind of people engage in dynamite business.

Ovi is grateful her flyers are in their persons, they surely will come round at some time- she has the week to ensure that.

Their cash box is full. They will have to make another.

CHAPTER 8

The day is slow. Iliy is having a well deserved late breakfast. Azeez stretch himself as if he has risen from sleep, and his bones cracked, in a way that was most irritating to Iliy, who returned to his food leaving Azeez idling at the wheel.

No passenger yet, and everywhere is quiet, until a man suddenly rush in to the car, surprising Azeez and Iliy.

"Drive- drive- drive!" screamed the passenger.

"Where?" asked Azeez.

The passenger doles out a lot of cash and hand it to Azeez.

"Get me out of town!" he ordered.

Iliy and Azeez freeze for a while. They can't understand what a smart looking middle-aged man with his left hand pressed to the side of his stomach mean by handing them such insane amount of cash just to drive out of town. This is out of town. Then they hear a gunshot, contain their bewilderment and drive off speedily.

What just happened, Azeez and Iliy try to comprehend. The passenger manages to have his correction lens covered in his dripping sweat. His breath seems to be parting from him.

"Anywhere specific you'd like to go sir? We are ways off town," Azeez said. "Sir?"

The Jetta grind to a halt. The sound of their heartbeat contends for dominance over the wailings of the unrelenting wind; leaves start to fill their windshield like rains should, seeking for morbid attention. The boys drop from the car and head for the backseat. The most benevolent man they ever met is lying lifeless at the back of their car. Judging from the heavy correction lens lying on the car mat, it's safe to say his vision had long departed him before his lungs followed; a visible gunshot wound can be seen now. The blood is not as red as they are used to seeing due to its mixing with the brown shirt of the man for a long time now.

The boys contemplate on what to do, which takes as much time as Iliy taking three regular steps each, back and forth.

Azeez opens the door at one end, while Iliy enters through the other way. They carry the body out of the car and into the bush. Azeez heads out to town to get shovels.

The sun has taken its position directly above Azeez and Iliy, blazing hot and forcing out as much sweat as possible from the boys who had buckets to give, over which they had no power to retain. A course of said sweat runs down across Iliy's right eye, making Azeez confuse it for tears. The boys look very weary and dirty now, staring down at the gravesite they just made for the man.

They return to their haven; Iliy's backyard. This is where the idea that the boys should dare out of town was agreed upon. It's less than two weeks and they've made more money than they've ever seen in their lives, and now a buried man to wonder about. The bounty on them takes an equal share of worry in their heads. They can turn to the police concerning what they know about the benevolent man, his family must be worried.

The white bed sheets left to dry on the clothes line keep smacking Azeez who is getting ready to have a smoke. Iliy is silently plotting their next move; life has played them to a corner taking with it the lights. The sun will become covered by thick clouds, ushering in a dark, breezy late morning ominous and unrelenting.

A phone starts ringing.

Both are a bit taken off since none of them own a phone. The sound of the ring is loud enough to aid the boys in finding it caught in the backseat. The man must have been the owner. Iliy is the first to retrieve it. They stare at the phone not knowing if to answer it, until it stops ringing. A different tone follows, this one not as lasting as the previous. Iliy reads the message.

"I can see the two of you. I know where you live. I know where your families live. Iliy, Azeez."

Surprise and anger come upon their faces.

The phone rings again this time Iliy press the receive button with the same resentment he hold towards this stranger.

"Iliy! You don't want to pick my call, that makes me feel sad," said the man in a husky tone, "you should show a bit of respect," he continued lacking authority.

Azeez has his cigarette lit, and is wondering why Iliy decided to hang on to the phone when they could both be in conversation with the unknown person.

"Respect who?" yelled Iliy. "The reason I am listening now is because I want to know what your game is."

Azeez lunges at Iliy to get the phone; if they can't be on at the same time, they can take turns. Iliy pleads for a second more with the stranger.

"Game, I don't play games," said the strange man, "I would like to watch a good game though, call me OG."

A heavy shock comes upon Iliy on hearing that name. His heart pounded a bit faster for a time, but the pale look on his face will make one think his heart stopped. Azeez gets a hunch that something abnormal is going on, his understanding of human expressions had afforded him the high street acumen that Iliy has undoubtedly come to rely on.

"The real OG?" Iliy try to wish the name away with a gentle tone.

Azeez get his own dose of shock; his newly lit cigarette comes to its end after a single drag. His heart begins to trample on him too.

The birds in the tree reach for greater heights leaving their nests behind. The white bed sheets become resistive to the pervading breeze as they reach a stand-still.

"I have not heard of any other OG around. You will tell me if you know someone moving around with that name right?" his voice carried the double features of subtle vulnerability and fiery disposition.

Azeez refrains from handling the phone.

"I do not know of one who would dare sir," replied Iliy.

"Good, that's just great. Good name is worth more than riches, do you read the bible boy?" he said in a friendly voice.

"Yes sir, I teach the kids at the bible school," Iliy falsely look to salvation.

"I like you boy, I feel at home with you, I see big things happening to you, and Azeez too, maybe you can come to the house sometime, I would like to show you around."

"Yes sir. Whenever is suitable for you," Iliy said without consulting his head.

"Oh today will be perfect," OG said before an abrupt pause. "You have my money."

"Uh!" Iliy said in hope of it sounding like a question to OG.

Iliy employs his poorly developed sign language skill in instructing Azeez to search the car for any cash.

"Come on boy don't grow just yet, stay an innocent kid, greed is for all devil's seeds," OG preached.

Azeez heads straight to where the money if any would most likely be, the spot where the benevolent man met his demise. With ease he finds a briefcase under Iliy's seat. The dying man must have worked his waning strength to tuck the case so well under the car seat. Azeez check what's in it, and then rushes to inform Iliy of the find. They could run now and create the world they've dreamed of. The allure of spending their twentieth birthday roving the planet; Iliy's first, then Azeez's three days later.

"We have it sir," Iliy said. He utilizes the phone's loudspeaker without an invitation from Azeez.

"You see I really mean it when I say you boys are special. Someone else does this he is found in pieces somewhere later," OG said calmly, "but I believe you boys will be of more worth alive. Now tell me I am not wrong."

"We are grateful for your believe in us," said Iliy.

"My boy, rest his soul," OG pause to pay respect, "charming

as he was, he lacked in survival instincts. You guys on the other hand are something else," OG goes silent, "I couldn't have asked for better... wanted criminals, educated, actors, I hear you guys know how to put up a good show," OG can be heard having a drink. "My daughter has been in forced custody of a small time thief Sully," urgency come on his voice, "normally I won't pay any mind to it, but this particular thief has a history of mental problems, people die quickly around him. I'm no angel, but if I must say, that boy is an evil genius, also desperate. And Azi is my favorite girl, her mama was a special kind of woman."

Azeez can almost guess where this is leading to- he has heard stories of OG's dilemma; you do his bidding you're damned, you go against his wish you're damned.
Iliy is in deep waters, for as long as he can remember he has never been this clueless.

"At noon you will meet him and make the exchange. But listen to me, say things don't go as planned, and anything happens to my girl, everything and everyone you love goes up in a blast, boom! So are you boys willing to undertake this mission for a father and daughter in distress?"

They really have no choice.

"Yes sir. It will be our pleasure," said Iliy.

"Azeez?" inquired OG.

"This will be my life work sir," answered Azeez.

OG cuts the line.

The boys stay quiet for a while not knowing what to say. How are they going to save someone from a ragtag kidnapping squad and come out clean? Azeez and Iliy have never considered themselves gangsters.

The phone rings again. Iliy picks it.

"Like all the great games in the world, they can be only one winner," OG's voice has grown deeper. "At the end of today, I want my daughter back to me safe and sound, and also I want to see him and whoever he is with as pile of ashes. That is the only result that will save you all."

The boys are shattered by the new demand. The

sun shines brighter, in contrast to their condition.

"Tough shit. Any idea this time?" asked Azeez, mockingly.

Iliy could only manage a nod. He doesn't have a plan.

"Not that they ever do us any good," said Azeez.

New birds have come to fill the abandoned nests, tweeting to Azeez's detriment.

Azeez's jolly grandfather and elusive mother, Iliy's sister and aunt are all the family they have in Colorful. In the world. The only ill they would have perpetuated against them was leaving Colorful without giving them notice. Even that was for everyone's good because they were always going to come back to share the spoils of chasing their dreams with them. No actor ever made it living in Colorful.

Iliy gets up from the dusty rock he has been sitting on and heads for the car.

"Mind your pocket," Azeez directed at Iliy.

Iliy checks absent-mindedly to see a scruffy flyer about to fall off from his pocket, which he reads.

Azeez laid his back on a rock, looking to see the pattern the sky has taken. He will say later that at this point he was trying to get a glimpse of Paradise- his heart seem to beat a bit regular when he turned his thought to this. The sky at this time of the year is mostly clear so it is the best time one can get to see into it. A world without OG will be close to Paradise for him; what if OG should die of a heart attack, get killed by a wronged member of society. They can ride into the sunset with their car boot loaded with cash and hearts full with dreams.

"Azeez I've found us a life-line," Iliy said excited, "and for the first time I think you are going to like this one."

Azeez joins Iliy to see if the prayers they are yet to offer have been answered.

CHAPTER 9

News about town is the demise of Mama Sunshine. People wailed, and rolled themselves on the floor, said a lot of great things about her. They did for a while. The feeling in the air was that the savvy and controversial Mama Sunshine will be disappointed in Colorful for engaging in all these pleasantries that does nothing to show her remarkable life.

San Thiaroye the son of Adare, the son of Baada the farmer that first witnessed the bomb-blast, who bore Honore the husband of Dorothy of whom was born Sunshine, was the first to suggest the DSSP were the ones largely responsible for her death.

Mama Sunshine might have put herself in harm's way by warning people not to drink water supplied by the government. Thanks to some pictures showing aliens having a drink in their spaceship which she got from her trip overseas to study for her teaching degree, she was able to convince the people that these same aliens provided the chemicals that the government put into all water wells.

The rise in sales of bottled water would mean good business for anyone in that trade- Mama Sunshine and Madam Social were the only ones in that trade. And looking at the said picture recently the aliens could easily be confused for men in costumes.

He further said the Secret Service did this by spiking the bonus twelve-pack of beverages she always receives for her patronage. It was a safe choice as they are not expected to be mixed with the regular drinks. Her four loyal workers on separate interviews confirmed that she was in the habit of drinking one of it and handing the rest to them; they all drank from it.

San Thiaroye in a last-ditch effort would offer that the drinks were tailored to her DNA but wouldn't say how he got to know for fear of his own life.

Madam Social was dragged into condemnation for employing the service of agents from District Six Secret Police to kill her bitter rival through carbon monoxide poisoning; it's a sure and clean way to go about it. District Six has stopped being a political classification for Colorful since the people petitioned for a suitable name that show their qualities or they close the factory at the time when the factory was still up and running, and most importantly one of the major source of revenue for Our government. Secret Police- well is a phantom, figures mothers conjure to scare their kids to stay indoors. It's always something with these people.

The boys were out of town and so no original conclusion from them.

The field they've been directed to looks serene, quite still, you wouldn't have thought of it as a den for erratic Sully and his cohorts; famed criminals. The quiet place is site for a proposed hotel that hasn't met completion. The building is five-storey long and the brilliant plan of the owner is quite evident in what has been accomplished so far. It is possible Sully will be in the top floor. The boys consider if it is necessary to go up to him.

"Is this the address you got?" asked Azeez. "What's worse is if this ends up being a setup. I'd hate to go to jail."

"Like a large scale drug type government sanctioned undercover exchange set up," Iliy said lightly.

"Exactly, they might be somewhere right now watching us, when we lose our guard, they are going to be all over us..." he said. "Freeze yous," Azeez joked.

"In the name of the government, freeze! To hell with all your rights you damn drug pushers!" Iliy added.

Azeez and Iliy laugh at their scenarios. The sun parks right above them, offering no succor for the boys. It's an extremely hot day. The sand aims to transfer some of its heat to the boys through their rubber shoes. The place is bare, no tree for shade. The boys return to the reality of the situation.

"Would you like to send a message to your people in case you die here?" asked Iliy.

"Make them have a feast, and when they are done,
tell them their poor son died rich in spirit and mind, next to the only family he ever needed," Azeez declared wasting no time.

"What if I am the last man standing, what do I tell your family?" he returned the favor.

Iliy is about to say something, when a terrible sound echo through the place.

Vulgar Sully wearing a sunshade and wielding a revolver comes out holding Azi tightly with her hands tied and eyes blindfolded. In a choreographed move Sully's cohorts appear, all stationed at the ground floor displaying their weapons. Eleven men ready to let fly their bullets on two unarmed teenagers.

Sully wore a matching denim jacket and trousers; Azi is scantily clad which will seem well suited for the heat bearing on Colorful today. Iliy could tell from her buttery skin and salient figure that she has to be as old as him. Azeez tries to see if Sully's eyes are red but the sunglass won't give in to his demand; that's his first effort in trying to read his adversary, he will attempt to know the man by talking to him.

Sully suffered from the weather, feeling the folly in his choice of fashion, he dashes forward pulling Azi along to get this business done quickly; the boys don't wait for an invitation as they pace forward like men about to start a fight. Both parties stop halfway from where they began.

"Who are you?" Sully lets out in an embarrassing croaky voice.

"Is there ever a reliable answer to that? If it's our name you mean its Azeez and Iliy," answered Azeez.

"Names- can you believe that boys?" Sully jeered, eliciting a huge laugh from his associates.

The breeze has given way for the sun, leaving the boys in

distress.

"What's your outfit?" asked Sully.

"We are the 'Lost Boys of the Purple Ribbon Society' we are always there, when there is no one left!" Iliy proudly said.

Sully lets go of Azi and walks to Iliy. On getting close to him, he takes off his sunglass to show the level of irritation that Iliy has caused him.

"That's the lamest thing I've ever heard. Have you wondered maybe there is a reason there is no one left?" Sully asked.

"Those words are not aimed at the ones who are leaving, neither does it concern why they might be leaving, just as long as there is still a need for our service," said Iliy.

"You educated types, you think you know better than everyone. You have an answer for everything right," said Sully.

"Hey, do you mind stepping back while we conduct business here?" Azeez take a note from Iliy's boldness.

Sully turns to leave and stops abruptly. Iliy receives a low blow from Sully's revolver. Azeez tries to charge on Sully, but the sound of gunshots he hear make him realize how powerless they are. He just managed to get Sully's attention who waste no time in hitting Azeez in the face with the butt of the same revolver. Both are on the ground clutching their wounds. Sully is having a swell time as he heads back to Iliy for unfinished business. Sully kicks him repeatedly in the stomach. Azeez is not left out, taking blows to the face over and over.

They are only saved by the ringing from their phone. Sully leaves Azeez and heads to where the sound is coming from- Iliy.

"What!" Sully screamed at the caller.

OG cannot be rushed.

"Now let's all be civil here, those boys have something for you from me. I only ask for the safe return of my girl- unharmed," OG cuts the call in his usual way.

Sully is disappointed in his handling of the situation; the business with the boys is working great for him, but he never got to say his piece of mind to OG. He begins to whimper for some injustice that he sensed has been done to him.

In my second and what turned to be my final day in captivity, I overheard one of Sully's talkative collaborators saying how the ransom will be used to increase the war effort against the system; top officials were going to receive visitations from Sully and his gang at random when he take the reins. He would make my father's era as crime boss a joke. His reign will introduce local operations, as opposed to robbing neighboring cities that is practiced now.

Azeez gets up and heads for the car. Sully excuses the long walk to the boot of the car as a result of the stress he put Azeez through. He lost his footing while returning with the briefcase, eliciting sympathy from Sully- for the sake of the briefcase.

Sully will go on to take the blindfold from my eyes and then indicate for me to count my steps to Iliy.

Azeez hands the briefcase to Sully, which he opens causing the trigger of a strange sound that Sully wasn't privy to; his visual acuity is the only one he employed for this moment. He smiled childishly at what he saw, the disloyal stack of money is also happy to meet its new owner.

Iliy unties the rope from my hands and signals Azeez.

The sound now known to be that of ticks get louder to Sully's collaborators as he gets closer to them.

Azeez is on a feverish race to catch up with Iliy and I.

The volume of the ticks is doubled and more urgent. I can't recall the expression on their faces at the time of the blast as the boys and I were a bit over five feet above the ground, but Sully's laughter was distinguishable from the sound of the bomb. It was the last thing he did with his intemperate life.

The briefcase was not rigged so well as to be inconspicuous to a close inspection. That was weighing on Azeez's mind on his way to get the briefcase from the car.

CHAPTER 10

Iliy and Azeez don't live in Colorful anymore. They have since become local heroes holding the respect and admiration of the people for their confrontation with the dreaded Sully and his gang.

Their infamous wanted poster is still being posted all over Colorful by unseen and unknown agents the people have come to suspect to be the always talked about Grey Hat Society Mama Sunshine hammered on before she met her end.

What a woman.

I have taken liberties with the stories to my discretion and satisfaction that such liberties will draw attention to the story. Most events occurred as I've written it.